The Cookie that Saved Christmas

Created by Billy Baldwin

Illustrated by Liesl Bell

Decozen Books, New York
dpbooks@optonline.net

Library of Congress Number: 2016917391
ISBN: 978-0-9791882-0-6

Decozen Books
P.O. Box 3238
Sag Harbor NY 11963
decozenbooks.com
dpbooks@optonline.net
Printed in Canada.

To my brother Ted, a true Cookiehead,
I miss you.

Dirk trudged up the hill to the place children were sent when they had nowhere else to go.

"Welcome to Crowsfoot Hill Orphanage. My name is Anna," stammered a small girl.

Dirk sniffed. The orphanage smelled like rotten cabbage and dirty wet socks.

After Anna showed him around, Dirk said, "Anna, it is Christmas Eve. Where is the tree? Why are there no stockings hung by the fireplace?"

Anna looked around nervously. "Quiet . . . Miss Crouch doesn't like Christmas. No one knows why," she whispered. "I stopped believing in Santa Claus a long time ago. . . ."

"But how will Santa ever find the orphanage if there's no Christmas spirit here?" Dirk asked.

Dirk's thoughts drifted away to a joyous Christmas Eve at his mother's bakeshop. They had made fruit cakes, cream puffs, and gingerbread treats. Dirk wondered if he'd ever have another Christmas as wonderful as that.

Later that night, Dirk couldn't sleep. Maybe a snack would help, he thought. As he snuck down to the kitchen, he stumbled into Anna, who was coming from the bathroom.

"You're not supposed to be roaming around at night," Anna warned.

"I need something sweet to lift my spirits," Dirk replied.

As she tried to tug him back upstairs, the two tumbled over, discovering a secret door.

"Dirk, you must go back to bed," Anna urged.

A blast of cold musty
air splashed Dirk's face.

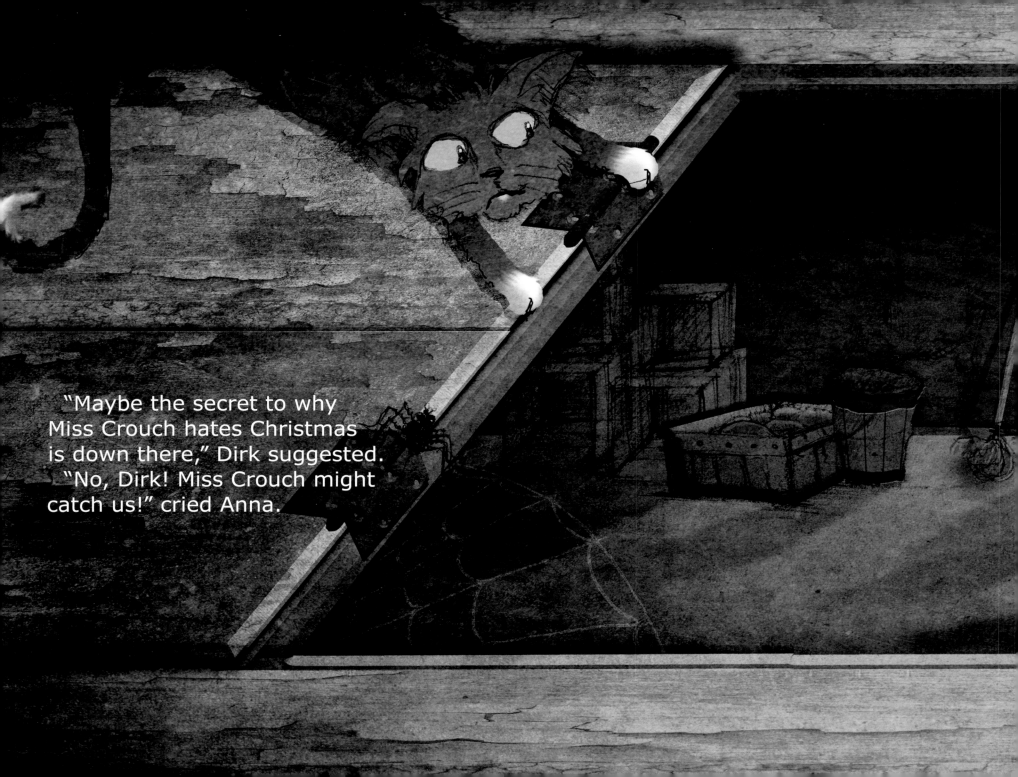

"Maybe the secret to why
Miss Crouch hates Christmas
is down there," Dirk suggested.
"No, Dirk! Miss Crouch might
catch us!" cried Anna.

They had been poking around the dusty basement for a few minutes when Dirk spotted an old newspaper article on top of a trunk of moldy Christmas decorations.

"Look! It's dated December 24th," said Anna. "Poor Miss Crouch was sent here on Christmas Eve."

HARBOR NEW[S]

24 December

Mr. and Mrs. Crouch of 18 Rosewood Drive have gone missing after their ship was caught in a sea storm. Their only daughter, Pamela Crouch, will be sent to live at Crowsfoot Hill Orphanage until they are found.

"That's why there's no Christmas spirit here," Dirk said. "We must bring it back to Crowsfoot Hill!"

Dirk picked up a strap of dusty old jingle bells as he curiously studied the old Christmas decorations in the trunk.

"But how? All we have is this box of rotting decorations, and we don't have money for gifts," Anna answered.

"I have an idea. Hurry! We have no time to lose!" Dirk said.

She followed Dirk into the kitchen, where he started measuring and mixing butter and eggs, flour and sugar, cinnamon and nutmeg. Then he showed Anna how to cut the dough into Christmas shapes. As they decorated the treats, Dirk and Anna could feel the magic of Christmas.
But time was running out.

They wrapped the treats and attached notes to each orphan that said, MERRY CHRISTMAS! FROM, SANTA. Dirk left a tray of treats for Santa, then went to deliver the rest of the gifts.

"What are you doing?"
Miss Crouch growled.
"Merry Christ—"

"Christmas gifts! There will never be Christmas in this house! NEVER!" said Miss Crouch. "Go to bed! I will deal with you two in the morning."

Just at that moment, Santa was on his way back to the North Pole. He caught a scent of something so sweet, so filled with Christmas spirit, that he couldn't help but follow it.

Inside, he found Dirk's treats, and his boots started dancing as he popped each treat into his mouth.

But Santa's Christmas joy turned to sadness when he
saw Dirk staring out the window, asking the night sky
why his love for Christmas could not change Miss Crouch.

With a twinkle in his eye, Santa hopped in his sleigh and flew away, leaving a magical trail of Christmas spirit.

On Christmas morning, Anna cried, "Miss Crouch, Dirk ran away!"

"Good. That will save me the trouble of sending him to work in the factories," said Miss Crouch.

"But Miss Crouch, Dirk was right. It worked!"

"What are you babbling about?" bellowed Miss Crouch.

Anna dragged her into the living room.

"Santa came to Crowsfoot Hill last night," Anna said.

"That's impossible!"
Miss Crouch said.
"I have to find Dirk."

Miss Crouch followed Dirk's
footprints in the snow and found
him shivering outside the church.

"Merry Christmas, Dirk! You were right, I still had some Christmas spirit left" said Miss Crouch, wrapping a warm blanket around him. Together they walked back to Crowsfoot Hill.

"Dirk, I found this gift for you under the tree," said Anna.

Dirk,

I hope this gift reminds you of a very special night. If you don't mind, I will call your tasty treats Christmas cookies and look forward to next Christmas Eve.

Santa

And from that day forward, on every Christmas Eve, Dirk, Anna, Miss Crouch, and the other children baked Christmas cookies that they shared with the whole town.

It became a tradition on Christmas Eve
to leave a plate of Christmas Cookies and
a glass of milk for Santa.